PICNIC

Robert Kraus

**WARNER
JUVENILE
BOOKS**
A Warner Communications Company
New York

Warner Juvenile Books Edition
Copyright © 1990 by Robert Kraus
All rights reserved.
Warner Books, Inc., 666 Fifth Avenue, New York, NY 10103
W A Warner Communications Company
Printed in the United States of America
First Warner Juvenile Books Printing: May 1990
10 9 8 7 6 5 4 3 2 1

Library of Congress Cataloging-in-Publication Data
Kraus, Robert, date.
    The Boogie Woogie Bears' picnic.

    Summary: After some initial tribulations, the Boogie
Woogie Bears have a rip-snorting, nit-picking Boogie
Woogie picnic.
    [1. Bears—Fiction.   2. Picnicking—Fiction]
I. Title.
PZ7.K898Bn   1990   [E]   89-51411
ISBN 1-55782-097-X

Come on down to the Boogie Woogie Bears' abode, Home Sweet Home. Dad is having his midmorning snooze. Shhhh. . . .

The Boogie Woogie Bears boogie on down to the picnic grounds where a surprise awaits them.

WE'D LIKE A TABLE FOR THREE BEARS.
I'M SORRY, BEARS, BUT THERE WILL BE A THIRTY-MINUTE WAIT FOR SEATING.
JUST LIKE THE BIG CITY.
I'M HUNGRY.
PICNIC GROUNDS

The Bears boogie on down to a little farm
at the edge of the woods.

Nobody's fenced in! Dad and the bull jump the fence
and head for the picnic grounds.
The Boogie Woogie Bears get their picnic spot.
The bull gets the cold shoulder.

YOU'R PICNIC SPOT IS READY, MR. BOOGIE WOOGIE! SORRY, NO BULLS ALLOWED!
PUFF
PUFF
PUFF
QUICK THINKING, TANGLETOOTH!

At long last the Boogie Woogie Bears
are about to have their picnic . . .
they think.

WHAT'S A PICNIC WITHOUT ANTS?
LET'S WATCH THE SUNSET, GEORGE.
PUT ME DOWN.
I'M AN ANT.
I'M AN UNCLE.

But while the Boogie Woogie Bears are admiring the sunset, the ants run off with their picnic basket!

Dad crawls under the fence to pat the cow...
which happens to be a bull.
The bull chases Dad across the meadow and round about.
Is Dad fenced in?
Is the bull fenced in?
????????????????????????

Mom is fed up.
Dad tries to look at the bright side.
Junior is hungry. What else is new?
Nothing else bad could happen.

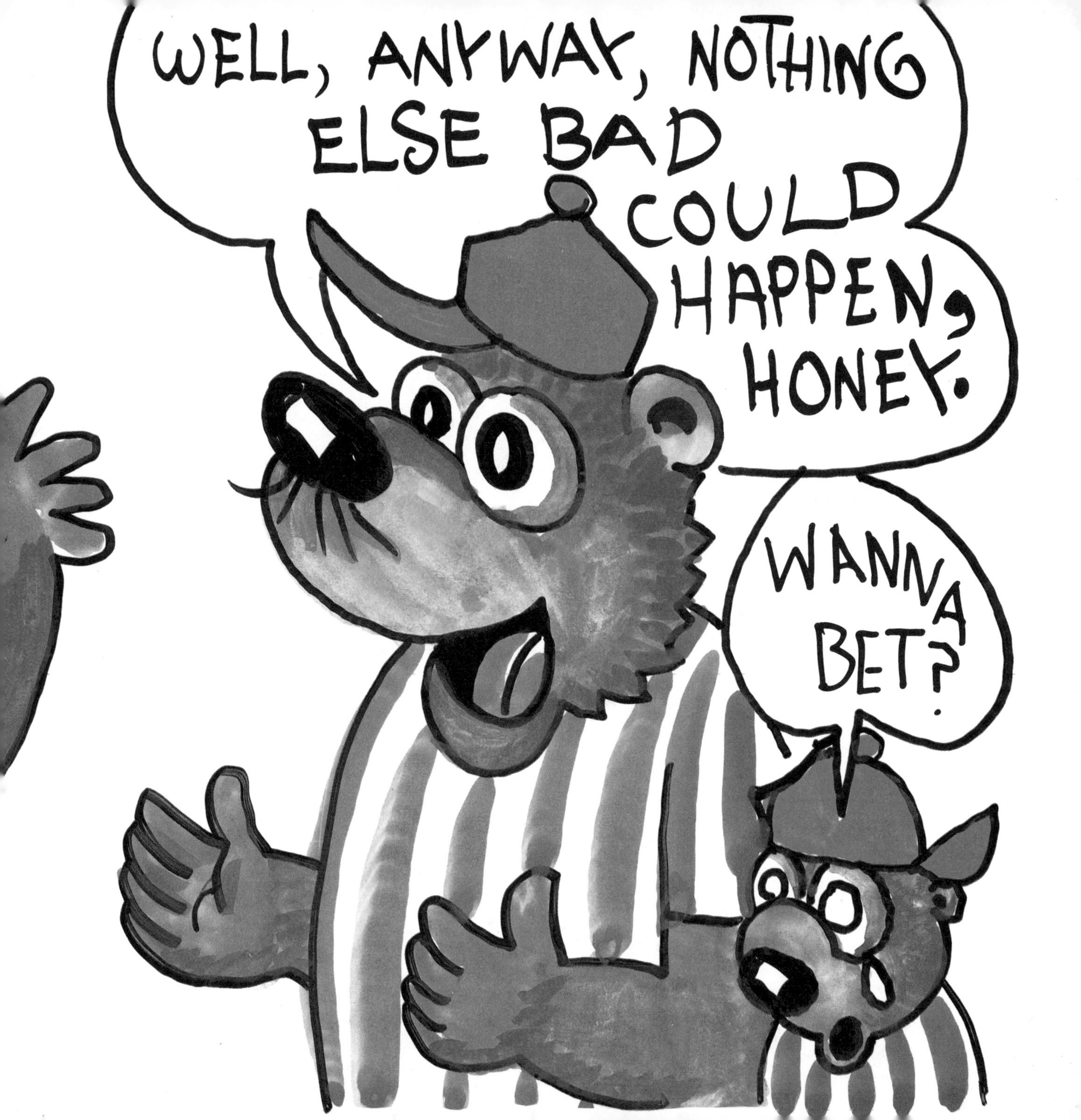
WELL, ANYWAY, NOTHING ELSE BAD COULD HAPPEN, HONEY.
WANNA BET?

But it does—and in buckets.

Well, finally the rain stops, and the ants begin feasting on the Bears' picnic. But they aren't having any fun. So guess what?

The ants pack up the picnic basket
and return it to the amazed
Boogie Woogie Bears.
Will wonders never cease?

IT'S THE ANTS WITH OUR PICNIC BASKET.
WHAT'S A PICNIC WITHOUT ANTS?
WE'RE SORRY.
I'M HUNGRY.
WHO KNOWS? WHO CARES?

Sooooo . . . the Boogie Woogie Bears and the ants and their furry and feathered friends have a rip-snorting Boogie Woogie picnic!

KIDS, HERE'S THE MORAL OF THIS TALE TODAY:
SHARING IS FUN THE BOOGIE WOOGIE WAY!
The End
YOUR FOREST FRIEND,
Tangletooth